For the Cat Club: Kaysi Weeks, Crystal Rice, Toni Milmoe,
Mandy Eisemann, Konyka Dunson, Jackie Malone,
Lori Smyth, Heather Smyth, and Chloe Martinez
—M.M.

To Niaina, the cat lover of the family.
Love you!
Auntie.
—S.C.

With thanks to Stephen L. Zawistowski, PhD, CAAB Emeritus, Adjunct Professor, Hunter College
Animal Behavior and Conservation program, for assistance in the preparation of this book.

Visit us on the Web!
rhcbooks.com

Educators and librarians, for a variety of teaching tools, visit us at RHTeachersLibrarians.com

Library of Congress Cataloging-in-Publication Data is available upon request.
ISBN 978-0-593-48319-0 (trade) — ISBN 978-0-593-48320-6 (lib. bdg.) —
ISBN 978-0-593-48321-3 (ebook)

MANUFACTURED IN CHINA
10 9 8 7 6 5 4 3 2 1
First Edition

How to Love a Kitten

by Michelle Meadows
illustrated by Sawyer Cloud

BEGINNER BOOKS®
A Division of Random House

On the farm,
we run and play.
I kick the ball.
It rolls away.

Under the porch,
I bend down low.
No ball in sight.
Where did it go?

A broken toy.

A silver pail.

Then something moves.

Is that a tail?

I call out, "Hey—
Look what I found!
Four kittens and
a cat curled round."

Grandpa comes.

He's here to help.

Mama Cat whines.

Kittens yelp.

Sky turns dark.

Here comes a storm.

"Let's get this family
safe and warm."

Grandpa lifts,
scoops up each one.
One by one,
until he's done.

The country vet
comes on the scene
to check the kittens
and the queen.

Checking noses,
ears, and throats.

Checking feet
and furry coats.

They need more food.
Not only that—
this Mama is
an indoor cat!

Purple collar.

Tag is missing.

Nails look trimmed,

and she's not hissing.

Setting up a
quiet room.
Kittens snuggle.
Kittens zoom.

Food and water.
Litter box.
Cozy blankets.
Catnip socks.

Hang up posters
all around
about the Mama Cat
I found.

Hurry, scurry,
fuzzy feet.

Meow! Meow!
It's time to eat!

Kittens growing
day by day.
Kittens tumble.
Kittens play.

Some bat toys,
while others hide.
They leap and pounce
and crawl inside.

One is missing.
Where are you?
In the closet,
in a shoe.

Round up all the
kittens now.

Meet my pony
and a cow.

Story time,
let's read a book.
The cow goes "moo,"
and kittens look.

Sleepy kittens
take a nap.
A couple curl up
in my lap.

Then one day . . .
phone rings at noon.
Mama Cat's owners
are coming soon!

They saw our signs!

Our job is done.

But maybe I

could keep just one?

Ding, dong. Ding, dong.
Visitors arrive.
Mama Cat's owners
meet all five!

Grandpa knows
what we should do.
Instead of one,
we will keep two!

They'll keep each other
company.
Like my new friend
will do for me.

Two for you
and two for me.
Dressed for a
kitten tea party!